The Bears' Den©
Published by Parrot Production Publishing Company LTD.

Registration Numbers TXU 649-106 - 9/22/94 PA 806-720 - 2/9/96
United States Copyright Office. The Library Of Congress.
ISBN 1-890571-29-6

*Dedicated to our elders,
whose experience and wisdom
we honor and respect*

THE BEAR'S DEN

Tootee's Magical Stories

by
Kambiz Azordegan

Illustrated by
Johnny Sajem

THE BEARS' DEN

Teaches:

the importance of family relationships and respect of elders.

To the Parents

Welcome to Tootee's Magical Paradise! Who is Tootee? Well, she's the most beautiful bird a child can imagine - and what could be more beautiful than that which comes from the mind of a child?

Tootee wants to help children grow up with beautiful, positive principles, so she flies from Land to Land collecting stories from all over the world to tell the children... stories that come from different cultures. Tootee always tells stories that bring to children positive principles for successful living, designed to encourage them to get along with one another, and to appreciate, respect and accept the differences that make each of us unique.

These principles are brought to life through friendly, animal-world characters and in a way that children enjoy, understand and imitate. In The Bear's Den, Banjoe, Bandee and Bamber, three lovable little bear cubs, experience some real fears and face difficult decisions, but in the end, they learn important lessons, as do all the characters in all of Tootee's stories.

The stories in the Tootee books are the same as those told in the Tootee's Paradise children's television programs that are enhanced with music and dance. The stories are also available on audio and video cassette so that children of all ages may enjoy and learn from them.

Live action version of this story
is also available on *video*.

My name is

_____

This is my book.
Will you please read it to me?

Deep in the forest, on the sunny slope of Rock Mountain, lived a very happy family of bears.

Mother Bear, Father Bear, and their three cubs — Banjoe, Bandee, and Bamber, lived together in their cave with Grandmother and Grandfather Bear.

Their cave kept them safe and warm throughout their long winter slumber, until the first rays of spring sunshine awakened them with a smile.

During the warm summer months, Mother and Father Bear went out every day to gather food for the family.

Grandmother and Grandfather were too old to roam the mountainside, so they stayed home to look after the cubs.

All morning long, the cubs romped and played outside.

They had great fun, chasing each other along the mountainside, jumping in the grass and climbing the trees near their home.

When afternoon came, the cubs would return home
to listen to Grandfather's funny stories.

"LET'S GO! IT'S STORY TIME!"

"I'LL RACE YOU TO THE CAVE!"

"LAST ONE THERE IS A ROTTEN EGG!"

Grandmother and Grandfather chuckled over the noise and excitement as Banjoe, Bandee, and Bamber tumbled over themselves getting into the cave.

They loved the cubs very much.

Grandmother smiled warmly as she greeted each cub with a piece of sweet, rich, honeycomb.

Grandfather sat in his favorite corner of the cave, waiting for the cubs to join him for story time.

Grandfather told wonderful stories about his travels to the sea and beyond.

He loved telling stories, especially the funny ones about catching fish.

Banjoe, Bandee, and Bamber loved listening to Grandfather's tales.

Time went on, and several summers passed.

One spring, the grandparents had trouble waking up from their long winter sleep. The rest of the family was busy cleaning the cave and getting ready for their first spring meal . . . .   But . . . *the grandparents were still asleep.*

Father Bear gently woke them up.

Then Mother Bear and Father Bear sat down to have a long talk with the grandparents.

Together, they decided it was time for the grandparents to go to the Bears' Den.

Father Bear explained to the cubs that sometimes, when grandparents get very old, they go to live in a sheltered place deep in the woods called the Bears' Den.

He explained, "There will be lots of older bears for them to pass time with, plenty of food to eat, and they will be safe."

The family traveled with the grandparents to their new home.
The cubs had never ventured so far from their cave, and they
were afraid of some of the things they saw.

There were dark places under the trees where no sunlight came through.

There were scary eyes flashing at them from deep in the underbrush.

As they neared the Bears' Den, they saw some older bears with scruffy fur and missing teeth.

Some were even missing an ear or a paw.

The cubs did not like this strange place

"Look over there, that bear doesn't have a left paw," Banjoe said.

"It's not polite to point, Banjoe," whispered Bamber.

"This place frightens me. I want to go home," Bandee cried.

The cubs said good-bye to their grandparents as quickly as possible and hurried away from that place as fast as their feet could carry them.

They were very quiet on the way home.

Sunny days came and went. One day Mother Bear announced that it was time to go visit the grandparents.

The cubs looked at one another and began to make excuses.

Bamber said, "I found a blackberry patch I'd like to visit today, Mother. The berries will be ripe by now."

Bandee said,
"I'm afraid I
must repair my
fishing gear
today, Mother
Bear."

Banjoe explained, "And I
promised my friend that I would
help him clean his cave."

Mother and Father Bear were not happy that the cubs didn't want to go, but they decided to let the cubs make their own decision about this first visit.

The problem was that the cubs made excuses every time Mother and Father Bear went to visit the grandparents.

Finally, Father Bear decided it was time for a family talk.

"I want to talk to you about why you don't want to visit your grandparents," he said.

"Oh, we want to visit them, we miss them very much," said Bamber.

"Then why don't you go with us?" Mother Bear asked.

The three cubs looked at one another, feeling a little embarrassed.

Bandee said, "We're really afraid of that place, Mother."

Banjoe continued, "That's the scariest place we've ever seen."

"I didn't know bears could be so scary," said Bamber.

Father Bear listened closely, then spoke gently.

"I understand why you're frightened by what you've seen at the Bears' Den. But you could try to set aside your fears and think about how your grandparents feel when you won't visit them . . . .

They miss you very much . . .

The cubs sat quietly and
thought about what Father had
said, and they knew in their
hearts that *he was right*.

In a few days, Mother Bear and Father Bear were ready once again to visit the grandparents.

This time, the cubs were ready to go.

"I've made a fresh blackberry pie for Grandmother."

"I'm taking my new fishing pole to show Grandfather."

"And I'm taking my hoe to help them with their garden."

The family set out happily on their journey.

There were still dark places and strange noises. There were plenty of scary sights, but the cubs were so eager to see their grandparents that they were no longer afraid.

When the cubs saw their grandparents, they let out whoops of joy.

Grandmother Bear hugged and kissed each cub with all her might, while Grandfather Bear beamed with happiness.

"I'm so happy to see you!" smiled Grandfather Bear.

And Grandmother Bear added, "I am so happy to have all my babies here together . . . .

We missed you
SO much!

After that, the cubs never missed a visit to the Bears' Den.

Banjoe, Bandee, and Bamber enjoyed every minute they spent with their grandparents. They learned to respect the wisdom of the older bears, who had lived much longer than they and knew much more about life. And they always enjoyed listening to their lessons and stories.

What have you learned?

_____

_____

_____

_____

_____

_____

_____

Which character do you like best? Why?

_____

_____

_____

_____

Questions

Why did Banjoe, Bamber, and Bandee make up excuses when told it was time to go visit their grandparents?

Why did the grandparents have a hard time waking up from their long winter sleep?

Why were the cubs afraid of the Bears' Den?

Did the cubs consider their grandparents feelings when they didn't want to go visit them?

Application

1. If you are ever afraid of anything or anyone, who would you talk to about it?

2. Why is it important to be considerate of the feelings of others?

3. Have you ever been around people that looked and acted differently from you? How did you feel? What did you do?

Live action version of this story
is also available on *video*.

Books & Video
Ordering Information
(800) TooTee P...aradise
(800) 866-8337